1914

CHANGES FOR
Rebecca

BY JACQUELINE DEMBAR GREENE
ILLUSTRATIONS ROBERT HUNT
VIGNETTES SUSAN McALILEY

THE AMERICAN GIRLS

KAYA, an adventurous Nez Perce girl whose deep love for horses and respect for nature nourish her spirit

1774

FELICITY, a spunky, spritely colonial girl, full of energy and independence

1824

JOSEFINA, a Hispanic girl whose heart and hopes are as big as the New Mexico sky

1854

KIRSTEN, a pioneer girl of strength and spirit who settles on the frontier

1864

ADDY, a courageous girl determined to be free in the midst of the Civil War

1904

SAMANTHA, a bright Victorian beauty,
an orphan raised by her wealthy grandmother

1914

REBECCA, a lively girl with dramatic flair
growing up in New York City

1934

KIT, a clever, resourceful girl facing the
Great Depression with spirit and determination

1944

MOLLY, who schemes and dreams on the
home front during World War Two

1974

JULIE, a fun-loving girl from San Francisco who
faces big changes—and creates a few of her own

Questions or comments? Call 1-800-845-0005, visit **americangirl.com**,
or write to Customer Service, American Girl, 8400 Fairway Place,
Middleton, WI 53562-0497.

Printed in China
09 10 11 12 13 14 LEO 10 9 8 7 6 5 4 3 2 1

All American Girl marks, Rebecca™, Rebecca Rubin™, and Ana™
are trademarks of American Girl, LLC.

PICTURE CREDITS
The following individuals and organizations have generously
given permission to reprint images contained in "Looking Back":
pp. 72–73—© Bettmann/Corbis (stitcher and boss); Jacob Rader Marcus Center of the
American Jewish Archives, Cincinnati campus, Hebrew Union College—Jewish Institute of
Religion (picket line); Library of Congress (strikers wearing banners); pp. 74–75—Kheel Center,
Cornell (ILGWU banner); Chicago Historical Society, DN-0001248 *Chicago Daily News*
photo (factory); National Museum of American History, Smithsonian Institution, Behring Center
(strike call); Kheel Center, Cornell (Clara Lemlich); Chicago Historical Society, DN-00056132
Chicago Daily News photo (police arresting woman); pp. 76–77—Brooklyn Public Library/
Brooklyn Collection (newspaper); © Bettmann/Corbis (Gloria Steinem, Bella Abzug);
© Reuters NewMedia Inc./Corbis (Ruth Bader Ginsburg)

Cataloging-in-Publication Data available from the Library of Congress

TO MY HUSBAND, MAL,
WHO SHARED THE KVETCHING
AND THE KVELLING

Rebecca's parents and grand-parents came to America before Rebecca was born, along with millions of other Jewish immigrants from different parts of the world. These immigrants brought with them many different traditions and ways of being Jewish. Practices varied widely between families, and differences among Jewish families were just as common in Rebecca's time as they are today. Rebecca's stories show the way one Jewish family could have lived in 1914 and 1915.

Rebecca's grandparents spoke mostly *Yiddish,* a language that was common among Jews from Eastern Europe. For help in pronouncing or understanding the foreign words in this book, look in the glossary on page 78.

TABLE OF CONTENTS

REBECCA'S FAMILY

PAPA
Rebecca's father, an understanding man who owns a small shoe store

MAMA
Rebecca's mother, who keeps a good Jewish home—and a good sense of humor

REBECCA
A lively girl who dreams of becoming an actress

SADIE AND SOPHIE
Rebecca's twin sisters, who like to remind Rebecca that they are fifteen

BENNY AND VICTOR
Rebecca's brothers, who are six and thirteen

UNCLE JACOB
*Ana's father, who has
brought his family all
the way from Russia*

AUNT FANNIE
*Ana's mother, who
hopes for a better life for
her family in America*

ANA
*Rebecca's ten-year-old
cousin, who is learning
to speak English*

JOSEF AND MICHAEL
*Rebecca's cousins, who are
fifteen and thirteen*

LILY AND MAX
*Two movie actors who
encourage Rebecca in
her love of performing*

MOVIE
ACTING

Rebecca cracked open a peanut shell
with her teeth. She munched the
peanuts, her eyes glued to the glowing
movie screen at the front of the theater. The piano
player near the stage plinked out a sweet melody
as the final scenes of *The Suitor* flickered to a close.
A large circle framed the two film sweethearts, then
grew smaller and winked shut just as the couple
was about to kiss. Boys in the audience whistled at
the romantic ending, and girls sighed.

As the piano player ended with a rousing flourish,
Ana leaned close to Rebecca. "It's so exciting. To
think that I am watching you on the movie screen—
with Max and Lily, too! I can hardly believe it."

1

Rebecca grinned. "I can barely believe it myself." She glanced at Max and Lily, sitting beside her in the theater, and thought back with pleasure to the day she had spent with them at Banbury  Cross Studios. When the director had needed a young actress to play the star's little sister, Rebecca had jumped at the chance. Her role was finished by the end of the day, but watching the movie now made it seem like everlasting magic.

The lights in the theater came on, and ushers strode down the aisle, making sure the audience left. "Everyone move to the exits!" the ushers called. They reached beneath the seats and pulled out a few boys who had tried to hide until the next show started.

As Rebecca moved into the aisle, she noticed some people staring curiously at Max and Lily as if the pair looked familiar. But without Lily's long, curly wig and Max's cap and gardener's clothes, no one quite recognized that they were the stars of the moving picture that had just ended.

"Thank you for taking us to see the movie," Rebecca said. "I couldn't imagine what it would look like, since I only acted in a few scenes."

"It's always a bit of a surprise to see how everything fits together when it's done," Max said.

Lily turned to Ana. "How exciting that Rebecca let you in on her secret," she said.

"I don't know how she can keep this to herself," Ana marveled. "I would want to tell *everyone* if I were in a moving picture."

"I wish my whole family could see it," Rebecca admitted. "But you know how my parents and grandparents feel about movies. They think acting isn't respectable, especially for ladies." Her voice faltered. "Someday I'll tell them . . . but I'm not sure when."

Lily smiled at Max mysteriously. "That's what secrets are all about," she said. "Exciting news that you can only share at the right moment."

Rebecca savored the memory of her acting role. "It doesn't matter if no one else ever knows," she said. "I loved being in that movie."

Their feet crunched over discarded peanut shells and candy wrappers as they made their way up the crowded aisle. Outside, the humid August air was thick

with heat. Lily waved a paper fan close to her face.

"I had forgotten how hot it is," Rebecca said. "The rest of the world just seems to disappear while I'm watching a movie."

"That's why moving pictures are so popular," Max pointed out. "They let people forget their troubles for a little while."

Lily took Max's arm as they turned to go. "We'll see you two at the Labor Day picnic next week," she said. "The whole studio crew is going, Rebecca, so you'll get to visit with everyone again."

"And don't worry," Max added. "We'll warn them that mum's the word about your movie role. Your secret is safe with us."

Rebecca hugged Max and Lily good-bye, and the girls headed down the bustling sidewalk to Ana's tenement.

"Max is right about forgetting all your troubles at a movie," said Ana. "If only my parents would go and enjoy themselves, instead of worrying all the time."

"What are they worried about?" Rebecca asked.

"Jobs and money," Ana answered. "Papa and Josef are not paid fairly at the coat factory. No one is.

The workers are asking for better pay. If the bosses don't agree, the workers might go on strike. Then Papa and Josef won't earn any money at all."

"Then let's hope there won't be a strike," said Rebecca. She knew Ana's family earned barely enough to make ends meet. Without Uncle Jacob and Josef working, the family would be in serious trouble.

Ana looked so worried that Rebecca wanted to cheer her up. "I've got a great idea," she said. "Let's act out a movie about a worker in a coat factory. Movies have happy endings, so in ours everyone will get a raise."

Ana perked up. "That sounds good! And since I know what the factories are like, I could play the boss."

The girls bounded up the front stoop and into Ana's tenement building. The smells of cooked cabbage and stale garbage filled the dark hallway, and the girls covered their noses and mouths with their hands, trying not to breathe. Straining to see, Rebecca followed her cousin up two flights of creaky wooden stairs. In the tiny, run-down apartment, Aunt Fannie had cleaned everything to a shine, and Uncle Jacob had painted the kitchen walls a sunny yellow.

"Where is everyone?" asked Rebecca, looking around the apartment.

"I don't know," Ana replied. "It's Sunday, so Papa and Josef have the day off. I guess they all decided to go out for a while. If we practice now, maybe we can perform our movie for them when they get home." Ana took one of her father's hats from a nail on the wall and plopped it on her head. "I'll be Mr. Simon. He's the boss." She draped her mother's shawl around Rebecca's shoulders and sat her at a small table in the tiny parlor. "You can be a poor stitcher who's just come to America."

"Okay," Rebecca said. "I'm Katerina Kofsky, fresh off the boat at Ellis Island." Rebecca bent over the table as if she were leaning over a sewing machine. "*Whirrrrrr*," she murmured softly, pretending to guide fabric under a needle.

"You really have to slump over," Ana directed. "Look as if you're too tired and hot to even push the fabric through."

Rebecca followed Ana's instructions, imagining that her shoulders ached from bending over the machine. She didn't need to imagine working in stifling heat, since Ana's apartment was so hot and stuffy, it didn't seem as if a factory sweatshop could be any worse.

Ana strode back and forth, her eyes fixed on Rebecca. "Faster! Faster!" she ordered. "You're too slow."

Rebecca really was sweating. She reached up and wiped the perspiration from her forehead.

"Aha!" Ana shouted, pointing an accusing finger. "You are not allowed to stop your machine without my permission, Miss Kofsky!" Ana pretended to pull out a notebook and write in it. "You will lose one hour of pay this week."

Rebecca clasped her hands together. "Please, Mr. Simon," she begged, "I was only wiping off my forehead so I could see the work better. Don't take any money from my pay. If my family can't pay the rent, the landlord will throw us onto the street!"

"And no talking!" Ana gave a mean smile. "I will be kind to you, Miss Kofsky, and only take out a nickel for talking instead of working."

"Not *more* from my pay," Rebecca cried. She leaned over and pretended to sew again. "Oh,

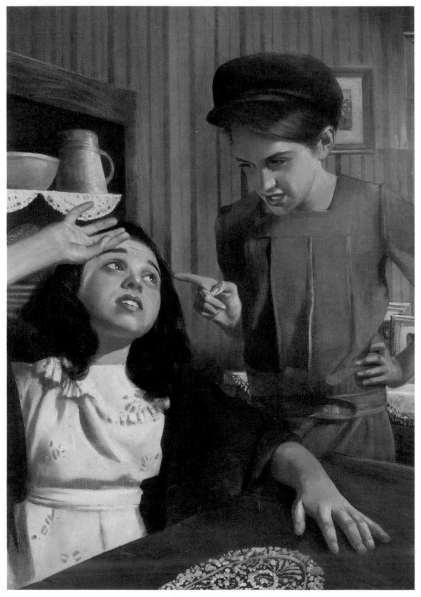

"You are not allowed to stop your machine
without my permission, Miss Kofsky!"

please, Mr. Simon. I am working hard."

"Still talking?" Ana made scribbling motions in her imaginary notebook. "That's another nickel! Soon you will learn to do what Simon says." She let out a nasty chuckle.

"What?" Rebecca was indignant. "How can you punish me for nothing? If you don't treat the workers fairly, we will walk out of this factory and go on strike. Then you'll be sorry."

Ana sneered. "Go ahead and strike. There are plenty more workers coming off the boat who will take this job in a minute. I don't need you or your complaints." She pointed to the door. "You do what I tell you, or you're fired."

Rebecca's heart was beating fast. No matter what she said, Ana seemed to get the better of her. Rebecca couldn't think of what to say next. "Why are you being so mean, Ana?" she sputtered. "In our movie, the workers are supposed to get a raise. You're not playing fair!"

Ana folded her arms across her chest. "I'm not Ana—I'm Mr. Simon. That means I can do whatever I want, and you have to go along with it."

Anger rose in Rebecca's chest. She couldn't do

anything without being punished. The movie wasn't fun anymore.

"CUT!" Rebecca yelled, so loudly that her cousin flinched. Rebecca pulled off the shawl. "Why are you doing this, Ana?"

"I'm acting in a movie, just like you said," Ana replied. "I'm being a factory boss."

"Well, you don't have to be so mean," Rebecca protested. "And so unfair."

Ana shrugged. "Josef tells me lots of stories about the factory, and that's how the bosses are."

Surely Ana was exaggerating, but Rebecca didn't want to argue. "Maybe we should play something else," she suggested.

Just then the door opened. Ana's mother and her brother Michael entered the apartment.

"How was picture show?" Aunt Fannie asked. "Someday I am going to see a movie for myself."

"Oh, Mama, it was wonderful," said Ana, her face glowing. "The movie seemed almost real, and the actors were so good. You should have seen Max and Lily and—" Rebecca nudged her cousin, reminding her of their secret. Ana's unfinished sentence hung in the air.

"While you were at the movies, we went to an important workers' meeting," Michael told his sister. "People gave speeches about how to make the clothing shops better places to work. If the bosses don't change things, there's going to be a huge strike." His eyes shone with excitement.

Aunt Fannie filled a glass with water and sat at the kitchen table. Her face was flushed with heat. "The hall is so packed, we must stand the whole time," she said, "but we stay and hear every word." She took a long drink and said to Ana, "Your papa and Josef, they are still at meeting. Workers from their factory are discussing what to do."

"An Italian girl talked about the Uptown Coat Company, where Papa and Josef work," Michael told them. "She said it was so hot this week, one of the stitchers fainted right onto the floor, but the other workers were not allowed to stop sewing and bring her some water." His voice rose. "When one girl left her machine to help, the boss fired them both!"

"Why would he do that?" Rebecca asked.

"He said they were wasting time instead of working," Michael said.

"These factories are not fit for human beings,"

Aunt Fannie said. "Things have to change, but all we hear is talk." She shook her head. "One young stitcher said the time for talking is over—now it is time to *do* something."

"That was Clara Adler," Michael said. "She's not much older than your sisters, Rebecca, but boy, does she have *chutzpah*. When she said the workers must walk out and *force* the bosses to make changes, everyone cheered." His voice was full of fire. "Clara shouted out, 'Either they change, or we strike!'"

Rebecca almost felt like cheering, too, just listening to Michael. If all the workers walked out together, that would show those bosses they couldn't get away with being so unfair! Then she remembered what Ana had said—the bosses could just hire new workers, and nothing would change. "Do you really think a strike would help?"

"It's the only thing left to do," Michael insisted. "Things can't get any worse than they are now."

"Yes, they can," Aunt Fannie said quietly. "If your papa and Josef can't bring home the pay every week, things will be a lot worse—for us."

INSIDE THE
FACTORY

On Monday afternoon, Ana and Rebecca
sat on the stoop in front of Ana's tenement,
hoping it might be cooler outside.

"They're going to have games and races at the
Labor Day celebration," Rebecca said. "If we practice
the three-legged race, maybe we'll win." She took
the ribbon from her hair and tied her right leg to
Ana's left leg. With their arms around each other's
waists, they tried to step in unison. At first they
stumbled a bit, but soon they began to pick up their
stride. Down the block they went, stumping along
and feeling so silly, they couldn't stop giggling. But
the heat was stronger than they were, and soon they
headed back upstairs for a drink.

"Come take a look at this shelf," Michael called from the fire escape outside the open parlor window. Rebecca peered out, wrinkling her nose at the pungent smell of paint and turpentine. Old newspapers covered the iron grate, and a freshly painted wooden shelf lay on top. Michael finished one last brush stroke and then swished his brush in a can of turpentine. He glanced up at the sky. "I don't know how this shelf will dry when the air feels wetter than the paint." He leaned back and looked at his work. "I think dark blue is the nicest color so far."

Rebecca admired the piece, which had three perfectly joined shelves and a swirly design carved at the top. "Are you going to hang it in the apartment?" she asked.

Aunt Fannie came over, wiping her hands on her apron. "Your Uncle Jacob is fine carpenter," she said. "He made that shelf for us." She pointed toward the kitchen, and Rebecca saw a sunny yellow shelf hanging on the wall over the work sink. It was just like the one Michael was painting. "Neighbors see this shelf and admire," Aunt Fannie went on.

"Then your uncle has genius idea to build shelves to sell to other renters."

"When we have a bigger place to live, my father will have a real work room, with plenty of space for his tools," Michael said. "Then he'll be able to make cabinets and tables, too."

Rebecca wondered how Uncle Jacob would be able to afford a larger apartment. If he got a raise, perhaps the family could move.

Michael started to clean up the newspapers when something grabbed his attention. "Look! Here's a picture of Clara Adler in the newspaper," he called, handing the wrinkled paper through the window.

"Let's see," Rebecca said, smoothing out the wrinkles and holding the paper up for Ana and Aunt Fannie. Clara did look quite young, but Rebecca detected a look of steely determination in Clara's eyes as she stood on a stage speaking to other workers. Rebecca glanced at the head-lines. "Honest Pay for Honest Work," read one. "Factories Are Fire Hazards," warned another.

Rebecca began reading. "Why, these are letters

that ordinary people wrote to the newspaper," she marveled. Each one contained a different opinion about the clothing factories. "Listen to this: 'Dear Editor, At my job we are not allowed to use the bathroom, except during our short lunchtime. Then so many girls are lined up, there is no time to eat, except while we stand and wait our turn for the bathroom.'" Rebecca looked up. "That's terrible. How could any place be so mean?"

"Clara Adler wants to change that by organizing the coat workers to strike," Michael said with admiration. "Now there's a girl who does a lot more than just complain!"

Aunt Fannie returned to the kitchen and finished packing food into two covered baskets. "I know that *our* workers will complain if we don't bring them something to eat tonight." She held the baskets out to Ana. "Take your father and brother their suppers before it gets any later."

"Why didn't they bring their suppers with them when they went to work?" asked Rebecca.

"Factory is too hot for food to sit out all day long," Aunt Fannie replied. "Without icebox, their suppers would spoil by evening."

Rebecca was curious to see if the factory was really as bad as Ana and Aunt Fannie described it. "May I go too?" she asked. Aunt Fannie hesitated, but Rebecca persisted. "I'll go home as soon as we deliver the baskets," she promised, and Aunt Fannie agreed.

Outside, heat radiated from the sidewalk, and Rebecca felt as if she were pushing against a wall of wet cotton. Damp ringlets of hair stuck to the back of her neck.

"I'm glad you're coming with me," Ana said. "I always feel a tiny bit scared when I go. As soon as I open the front door, the noisy machines sound like growling animals."

"It can't be that bad," Rebecca declared. "My parents worked in a shoe factory when they first came to America, and Mama jokes about it. She says that she and Papa fell in love over a pile of shoes, and that's why they are a perfect pair."

Farther up the block, Rebecca noticed a river of water running down the gutter next to the sidewalk. When the girls turned the corner, they saw a gushing fire hydrant. Kids of all ages were splashing in the water, shouting and squealing with delight. In

With a whoop, the cousins darted into the spray and
gasped as the cold water hit them.

the middle of the street, a horse pulling a delivery wagon had stopped to drink from a shallow puddle.

"An open fire hydrant!" Rebecca exclaimed. "Let's run through and cool off!" Ana didn't need to be convinced. With a whoop, the cousins darted into the spray and gasped as the cold water hit them.

"My stockings are soggy, but it feels wonderful!" Rebecca said gleefully as they left the boisterous hubbub behind.

"I'll bet this is the hottest day of the whole summer," said Ana. "I think I'll sleep on the fire escape tonight. It's much cooler than sleeping in the tenement. Lots of kids sleep outside, so it's almost like a party." Her eyebrows lifted. "Maybe you could sleep over tomorrow night!"

Rebecca's eyes lit up. "Oh, I hope Mama will let me!" She imagined what it would be like looking at stars overhead as she went to sleep.

After several blocks, Rebecca saw a tall brick building ahead. It cast a deep shadow across the sidewalk and street. A huge sign on the building read UPTOWN COAT COMPANY.

Ana pulled open the heavy metal door, and the cousins stepped into the gloomy entryway. Carefully, they climbed up six steep flights of rickety stairs. A humming noise, like a swarm of angry bees, grew louder as they approached the top.

"I can see why you don't like coming here," Rebecca admitted. "This place gives me the willies." A thick blanket of heat pressed against her, and Rebecca felt as if she couldn't breathe. But she had come this far, and she wasn't going to turn back now.

Ana pointed to a door. Black letters painted on the smoked glass said PRIVATE—NO ADMITTANCE.

"That's Mr. Simon's office," Ana said, speaking loudly into Rebecca's ear so that she could be heard above the sound of buzzing machines. "Josef says he has nice big windows in there and a fancy electric fan right on his desk." Rebecca followed Ana toward a solid metal door at the end of the hallway. "That's where my papa works and where Josef picks up bundles to deliver."

The metal door opened with a grating sound, and a stooped man staggered out, balancing a heavy pile of coats on his back. The door thudded shut behind him, and Rebecca moved out of his way.

20

Ana rushed forward. "Josef!" she cried.

Rebecca couldn't believe it was Ana's brother. His face was lined and his skin looked pasty gray. He nodded at them as he shuffled by.

"We've brought your dinner," Ana said, but Josef didn't answer. He struggled down the steep staircase trying to carry the load of coats.

Rebecca remembered Ana playing the boss and fining her just for talking. Would Josef have money taken from his pay if he just said hello to his sister?

A balding man with a potbelly stepped up to them as the girls opened the metal door to the workroom. "No kids in here," he barked. "Too dangerous." He snapped his suspenders against his chest.

Rebecca stepped back, covering her nose and mouth. The sour odors of sweat and machine oil blended into one foul smell. She would never have believed that the smell and the heat could be worse than in the tenement. Inside the huge loft, men with curved knives leaned over wide tables. They sliced swiftly through layers of thick fabric, their hands nearly a blur. Endless rows of young women in long-sleeved

21

different factory, it would be just as bad. Maybe someday they will be able to leave . . ." Her voice trailed off.

There was nothing else to say. As terrible as the factory was, Rebecca understood that Uncle Jacob and Josef needed their jobs. They were trapped, like the other workers.

Rebecca remembered the steely glint in Clara Adler's eyes. Complaining wouldn't change anything. Something had to be done.

CHAPTER
THREE

CITY TREE
HOUSE

On Tuesday, Rebecca ate her lunch as fast as she could and finished all her chores in record time. In spite of the heat, she felt a shiver of excitement as she stuffed her pajamas into her calico bag. Tonight she was going to sleep out on the fire escape with Ana.

"This is going to be the best day of the week," she exclaimed.

"Don't forget these." Mama handed Rebecca her toothbrush and a tin of tooth powder. Rebecca dropped the items into her bag and quickly tucked in a folded piece of paper. The paper held a secret she was going to share with Ana when they were alone.

"It's clouding up," Mama said. "Maybe we'll finally get some rain."

Rebecca groaned. "That would spoil everything!" She hurried to the door, clutching her bag. "On the other hand, now that I think about it, who cares if it pours? I'm so hot, I'd love to get caught in a thunderstorm. *Oooh*—wouldn't it feel delicious?"

Mama just shook her head and gave Rebecca a kiss good-bye. "You two be careful on the fire escape," she cautioned. "I want you home tomorrow safe and sound!"

By the time Rebecca knocked on Ana's door, the threatening clouds had thinned and a few rays of pale sunshine struggled to break through the humid haze.

If only there were more windows in the tenement, it would be a little cooler inside, Rebecca thought as she entered Ana's stifling apartment. But tonight it wouldn't matter. She and Ana would be outside, breathing the fresh night air.

"How about making some lemonade?" Aunt Fannie asked, placing a sack of overripe lemons on the table. "Maybe a drink will cool us off."

Ana took a glass juicer from a shelf, and Rebecca

sliced lemons in half while Ana rotated each piece back and forth across the pointed tip of the juicer. The lemons were squishy-ripe with a few brown spots, and Rebecca guessed that Aunt Fannie had gotten them from a street peddler at a bargain. Tart, frothy juice dripped into the bottom of the glass dish. When it was filled, the girls carefully poured the juice into a pitcher through a fine sieve that caught the seeds. They mixed in water and sugar and took turns stirring until the sugar dissolved.

Ana chipped a chunk of ice from the block in the icebox and dropped it into the pitcher. "I really need a *cold* drink!" she said.

"Don't waste ice," Aunt Fannie scolded. "It's bad enough in this heat that I have to pay iceman every day. Maybe you believe old stories that in America, the streets are paved with gold!"

Aunt Fannie brought out a loaf of dark bread. "It is too hot to cook, so I hope a light supper will be enough." She took a jar of pickled herring from the icebox and began slicing some tomatoes. Rebecca hoped the small meal was really because of the heat, and not because Aunt Fannie couldn't afford anything more.

Supper was over quickly. After Rebecca
and Ana washed and dried the dishes,
they helped Michael cover the opening
to the emergency stairs on the fire escape
with some boards.

Michael glanced up at the cloudy sky. "If you
two sleep out tonight, you may get a good bath,
too." He made sure the boards were firmly in place
and then grinned mischievously. "If you don't get
washed away by a thunderstorm first, this should
keep you from falling through." He leaned over the
edge of the railing and gave a long whistle that got
lower and lower in pitch. "It's a long way down."

Ignoring her brother's teasing, Ana climbed
back through the window and dragged a feather bed
from a corner of the parlor. She pushed while
Rebecca pulled it through the window and onto the
fire escape. Aunt Fannie handed out a sheet and two
soft pillows. Up and down the block, Rebecca saw
other children setting up beds outside. They began
to banter and call over the railings.

"Catch!" a tall girl in the next building shouted
to Ana. She tossed a red rubber ball across the space
between them. Ana caught the ball in both hands

and then tossed it back. The game lasted until the ball was missed and went tumbling down, bumping against jutting fire escapes until it hit the pavement below.

"Finders keepers!" shouted a skinny boy playing on the street. Then he laughed. "Just kidding." He heaved the ball as high as he could, and it bounced onto the girl's fire escape.

When it began to grow dark, Rebecca and Ana slipped into their nightclothes and nestled into the feather bed. "I feel like I'm floating in the sky," Rebecca said. "This must be what a tree house is like."

"Exactly like a tree house," Ana laughed, "except for the tree!"

The girls settled into the cool bedding, and Rebecca felt a light breeze riffling the air. Across the street, someone began singing.

> *In the good old summertime,*
> *In the good old summertime,*
> *Strolling down a shady lane . . .*

A wheezy accordion began to play along, and more neighbors joined in the song. Soon the melody drifted from fire escapes and rooftops up and down the street, with a few brave voices harmonizing.

You hold her hand and she holds yours,
And that's a very good sign
That she's your tootsey-wootsey
In the good old summertime.

Rebecca heard the kitchen door opening and heavy footsteps inside. She peered through the open window and saw that Uncle Jacob and Josef had just come home. Rebecca knew from working at Papa's shoe store how tiring it was to work even until suppertime. It was so dark now, it had to be close to nine o'clock. How could her uncle and cousin work such long hours every day? They must feel exhausted.

"Would you like tea?" Aunt Fannie asked softly.

"It's too hot to fire up the samovar," Uncle Jacob said. The icebox door opened.

samovar

"That lemonade looks wonderful, though."

Glasses clinked in the kitchen. Josef washed at the sink and then pulled a feather bed from under the sofa, where Michael was already asleep. Josef lay down and began to read a book.

"We've got another long day tomorrow," Uncle Jacob told him. "It's good to read, but now you need to sleep."

"I know, Papa," said Josef, "but I've got to keep learning English, or I'll be carrying bundles of coats the rest of my life."

Uncle Jacob sighed. "The heat in the workroom has been unbearable," he told Aunt Fannie. "But Mr. Simon keeps shouting at us to work faster. Ever since the meeting on Sunday, everyone's whispering about going on strike." His voice trailed off as he headed to the bedroom. "I don't know, Fanya. I just don't know . . ."

Aunt Fannie sounded alarmed. "I've heard so much about strikers being attacked on the picket line. Would you be able to watch out for Josef?"

"You know I'd do my best," he promised.

Later, after Josef had finally turned out the light and gone to sleep, Rebecca gave Ana a nudge.

"Are you awake?" she whispered.

"Yes," Ana said. "My nightgown is sticking to me like wet paper."

Rebecca unfolded the letter she had been hiding and handed it to her cousin. Ana squinted in the glow from the streetlamps. "Why, it's addressed to the newspaper editor," she said softly. Her eyes widened as she read. "Oh, Rebecca!"

"If people realize how awful it is inside the factory, then surely the city will change the laws," said Rebecca. "That will make the bosses treat the workers fairly, and no one will have to go on strike."

Ana shook her head sadly. "It's a good letter, but there have been dozens of letters in the newspaper already, and nothing ever changes."

Rebecca felt a sinking feeling in her chest. "Maybe if everyone who agreed with us wrote to the newspapers, there might be so many letters that the mayor would see them and realize he has to do something."

"I suppose it's possible," Ana agreed, but she didn't sound convinced. "Michael says the factory owners are more powerful than the mayor, so they

Ana's eyes widened as she read. "Oh, Rebecca!"

do what they want." She patted Rebecca's arm. "But thanks for trying."

Rebecca tucked the letter under her pillow and lay back, looking through the railing onto the street below. Grown-ups sat on the stoops talking and fanning themselves. Young couples strolled along the sidewalks. Lots of them worked at the factories themselves or knew people who did. *What if they all wrote letters,* Rebecca wondered as she closed her eyes. *Tomorrow I am going to mail my letter to the editor. Maybe it will help.*

⚜

The metallic screech of braking trolleys woke Rebecca with a start. She blinked her eyes open to another hazy morning. The kitchen door creaked shut, and she realized that as late as Uncle Jacob and Josef had come home from work last night, they were already up and leaving again. She rubbed her eyes. The street below was bustling with horse-drawn wagons. Peddlers pushed loaded pushcarts in front of them, heading for their favorite spots. Newsboys shouted out the headlines. "Labor

34

problems at Uptown Coat—read all about it!"

Ana sat up and looked at Rebecca with alarm. "That's where Papa and Josef work," she breathed. Rebecca nodded silently.

The girls scrambled inside through the window, dragging their bedding after them. They stored the feather bed in a corner of the parlor and then helped Michael lay down newspapers on the fire escape. He brought out three unpainted shelves and a fresh can of paint. They watched him brush a shelf with mint-green paint as the newsboys shouted on the street below. The air had cooled slightly overnight, and a sultry breeze was stirring.

"The coat factory workers are about to go on strike, and all I can do is paint shelves," Michael muttered. He kicked at the railing in frustration. "I'm not helping at all." Rebecca knew how Michael felt. There seemed to be so little that anyone could do.

The girls went in to wash and dress. They ate their breakfast rolls in silence at the kitchen table while Aunt Fannie filled the metal work sink with water. She began to scrub clothes against a washboard, making a steady rhythm as lather slid down her arms.

Michael leaned his head in. "How about helping me out?" he called from the fire escape. "I want to get these done this morning, in case it really does rain."

The girls climbed back outside, and Rebecca chose a shelf to paint. She tried to keep her brush strokes even as the pale green paint glided over the graceful curlicues carved into the smooth wood. *Uncle Jacob is such a good carpenter,* she thought. *He should be building cabinets and furniture all the time, not cutting cloth in a sweatshop.*

The morning slipped by as the three painters bent over their work. After a while, Ana stretched and rubbed her back. "So much bending," she complained. "I need a break—before *I* break!"

"You haven't finished that shelf," Michael said, but he put down his brush and stretched his arms. "I guess I could use a drink of water," he admitted. "Good thing we don't work in a factory!"

"Mrs. Rubin! Mrs. Rubin!" a woman called breathlessly from a nearby window.

Aunt Fannie poked her head out, wiping her wet hands on her apron. *"Nu?"* she asked in Yiddish. "What is it?"

A stream of Yiddish poured from the woman. She was talking so fast, she could hardly catch her breath. "It's the coat factory, Mrs. Rubin! The workers are pouring into the street. They've gone on strike!" Aunt Fannie covered her mouth with her hand.

"Get your hat," yelled the woman. "We're going to march on the picket line."

Aunt Fannie pulled off her apron as the girls scrambled inside.

"Don't go, Mama," Ana pleaded. "There's nothing you can do. Just wait, and Papa will come home."

Aunt Fannie set her mouth in determination. "Papa and your brother are marching with their fellow workers," she said, "and I will stand beside them."

"I'll come, too," Michael said, leaving his painting. "This can wait."

"No," Aunt Fannie said firmly. "You stay here with the girls. Ana, you and Rebecca will please finish the laundry and hang it up inside." She pinned on a hat, poking in two long hatpins, and took an umbrella from underneath the sink. "A picket line is no place for children."

"What if we stayed right next to you?" Rebecca asked her aunt. "Wouldn't we be safe then?"

Aunt Fannie put her hands on Rebecca's shoulders and looked at her steadily. "The bosses hire men to break up the strike. It gets dangerous." She rushed out the door, calling, "Don't leave here before I get back."

As soon as Aunt Fannie had gone, Michael turned to the girls. "I should be there, too." He pounded his fist against the wall. "I should be doing more to help—much more."

"You're painting shelves to help Papa earn extra money," Ana said kindly. "It's just as important."

"It's not enough," Michael said bitterly. "Not when Josef has to work so hard. It's not right that I go to school and he can't."

Rebecca felt the letter in her pocket. Maybe Ana was right. Writing to the newspaper wouldn't help enough.

Michael's voice rose. "The more people who protest, the better the chance that the bosses will give in."

That was just what Rebecca had been thinking.

"Then we should all go," she said. She had heard Papa talk about other companies that paid better wages and made their factories safer only because the workers had gone on strike. She turned to Ana. "If letters in the paper won't change things, maybe the strike will."

"Mama told us not to leave," Ana argued.

Rebecca knew she shouldn't disobey her aunt, but Michael was right—staying home wouldn't help win the strike. She wondered if Michael would have to work in the factory as soon as the law allowed him to quit school. He was almost fourteen. And what about Ana? Would she have to learn to sew on the noisy machines? The memory of the young stitcher with the pale skin and dull eyes still haunted Rebecca. She couldn't bear the thought of Ana working in such a place.

"If a strike will get people's attention and help change things for the better, then I think we should go," Rebecca said hesitantly. "Papa always says we all have to try to make the world a better place. He and Grandpa tell us *tikkun olam*—'repair the world.' We have to do our part, Ana, even if it might be dangerous."

Michael nodded. His mouth was set in a
determined line. Rebecca looked questioningly at
Ana, who hung back against the sink full of laundry.
The soapy bubbles had burst and a slick film lay
across the dingy water.

"I'm afraid to go," Ana said hoarsely.

"Getting out of Russia was more dangerous
than this," Rebecca pointed out. "You have lots of
courage, Ana."

Ana shook her head. "Not enough for this."

"Courage comes when you need it," said
Rebecca. "I know you want to help your father and
your brother. This is our chance!"

The uncertainty faded from Ana's face. She let
out a deep breath. "Let's go."

Michael reached for his cap as Rebecca opened
the door. She felt a prickle of fear at what she was
about to do. Ana, Michael, and Rebecca stepped into
the dark hallway, and Ana closed the door behind
them. The click of the lock reminded Rebecca that
she couldn't turn back.

A LOSING
BATTLE

A few blocks from the coat factory,
Rebecca heard a raucous din, louder
than the factory machines and louder
than the thunder that rumbled across the sky.
As Rebecca, Ana, and Michael drew closer, the
noises became more distinct. Feet stomped against
cobblestones. Angry voices cut the air like punches.
"Strike! Strike!"

The factory building came into view, surrounded
by a surging crowd of men and women. Many of
the strikers walked with linked arms, while others
held signs high above their heads. Rebecca saw signs
written in English, Yiddish, Italian, and Russian.
"We Shall Fight Until We Win," read one. Another

said "In Unity Is Our Strength" in red paint. There was a sense of warm camaraderie, but the strikers looked determined.

Rebecca reached for her cousins' hands. She scanned the marchers, searching for Ana's family, but the faces blurred together like a movie reel running too fast.

A loud horn blared, and a sleek black motorcar sped up to the curb. Men wearing caps with wide visors pulled low over their eyes jumped out and rushed into the mass of strikers. From under their jackets they pulled short, thick wooden clubs.

"Goons!" Michael shouted above the noise. His hand tightened on Rebecca's. "Stay back!"

The thugs filtered into the crowd. One fell into step behind a striker and suddenly whacked the backs of her knees with his club. The woman fell to the street, crying out in pain. As the thugs tripped and pushed the marchers, some of the women pulled out their hatpins and jabbed the goons. Others used their umbrellas to hit back. Rebecca wondered if that was why Aunt Fannie had used two hatpins and taken her umbrella along.

Within moments, it seemed that everyone was

fighting or shoving. Rebecca, Michael, and Ana
slowly backed away, watching in horror. Overhead,
thunderclouds rolled across the sky, blocking the
daylight and turning the street almost as dark as
night. Above the tumultuous din, Rebecca heard
the clatter of hooves and the clang of bells as horse-
drawn wagons raced up the street.

"It's the police!" she shouted with relief. "Now
they'll arrest the goons and protect the workers."

Blue-uniformed policemen clambered out of the
wagons, blowing their whistles. As Rebecca and her
cousins watched in disbelief, the police ignored the

thugs and collared the strikers instead.

"What are they doing?" Rebecca cried. "They're hitting the strikers with nightsticks and dragging them away, even if they're hurt!" She remembered Ana telling her that the factory owners had power in the city. Had they gotten the police to help break the strike?

"We've got to find Mama," said Ana. She broke away and nearly disappeared into the crowd before Rebecca and Michael pulled her back.

Just ahead on the street corner, a young woman stepped onto a wooden soapbox and began to address the crowd. Her voice carried above the uproar, and in spite of the melee people stopped to listen. Rebecca thought she looked familiar. Was she a stitcher at the coat factory? But this girl's eyes weren't dull and lifeless—they gleamed with strength and hope.

"It's Clara Adler," Michael cried, "from the workers' meeting!" Rebecca strained to hear.

"I am one of you," Clara shouted, and the strikers sent up a cheer. "We work hard for our bosses, and all we ask is to be treated fairly in return." Clara's voice was full of passion, and Rebecca felt her heart swelling with admiration.

Clara continued. "Every worker deserves—" In mid-sentence, two thugs kicked the soapbox from under her. Clara toppled to the cobblestones, and they dragged her away. The crowd surged forward, pulling Rebecca and her cousins along. Rebecca stumbled against a hard object and discovered it was the wooden box that had been Clara's miniature stage. Banging into the crate seemed to knock an idea into Rebecca's head. She stepped onto the soapbox and fumbled in her pocket for her letter. Could her thoughts encourage the strikers?

"Many workers head to the factory every morning before sunrise and work hard into the night to feed their families," Rebecca read in a loud voice. Those closest to her fell silent, and in a moment she was speaking to an attentive audience. "But they aren't paid fairly. The bosses have to make their jobs better—the hours shorter—and the factories safer!" There was a burst of applause. Rebecca was about to continue when she felt a sharp, stabbing pain as a rock struck her head. The letter flew from her hand.

Dark spots clouded her sight, and she crumpled to the street.

When Rebecca opened her eyes, she was in an alleyway. Michael's and Ana's frightened faces peered at her, and the commotion of the strike sounded like a distant echo.

"Can you stand up?" Michael asked, trying to help Rebecca from the street. "We'll never find the others now, and we've got to get you home."

Rebecca struggled to her feet. Images swam dizzily before her eyes. Her head throbbed. Blood had splotched her dress. With Michael and Ana supporting her on both sides, she staggered from the alleyway. A bolt of lightning lit the sky and a thunder-clap shook the air as a torrent of rain hammered down. The rain splashed against the cobblestones and streamed down gutters. Rebecca turned and glanced at the chaotic scene behind her. Through the dim light and pouring rain, she glimpsed two familiar figures being roughly pushed into a police wagon. It was Uncle Jacob and Josef.

❧

On Thursday, Rebecca felt as if she had awakened from a dream. She gingerly touched the bandage Mama had put on the night before and tried not to wince.

All morning, neighbors and family streamed into the apartment, asking about Uncle Jacob and Josef and fussing over Rebecca's injury. Still feeling dizzy, Rebecca sat on a chair in the parlor. She was glad when Michael and Ana arrived.

"What were you children thinking, going off to a picket line?" Mama scolded.

"We wanted to help," said Michael.

"We didn't think anyone would get hurt," Ana added. She looked as though she was on the verge of crying. Rebecca winked at her and saw a tiny smile of relief.

"I'm glad we were part of the strike," Rebecca said. Her voice filled with conviction. "I really am, Mama! Just believing that something is wrong isn't enough. I had to do something about it, and this seemed like the right thing."

Rebecca's grandmother threw her hands in the air. "Not only going to picket line, but making a speech, yet!" Bubbie cried. "What if that rock had hit your eye? Stirring up trouble is a dangerous business. When you find hornet's nest, you don't poke it with stick!"

Rebecca was relieved when Mama and Bubbie went back into the kitchen to fix tea. She needed time to think, without everyone scolding her. Maybe they were right—maybe it had been foolish to go to the strike. It certainly had proved to be dangerous. Most of all, Rebecca was sorry that they hadn't accomplished anything by going. Dejected, she scuffed her shoe against the chair leg.

Rebecca felt someone lifting her chin, and she looked up into Lily's pert smile. "How's my favorite kidlet?" Lily asked softly, perching on the arm of the chair. "Don't you worry a bit about that cut ruining your movie face. Even if the scar doesn't fade, your hair will hide it. You're still going to knock 'em dead with those beautiful eyes."

Rebecca flushed. She knew Lily was just kidding to raise her spirits, but the mention of movies reminded Rebecca that going to the strike was not the only thing she had done that was sure to upset her parents and grandparents. That is, if they ever found out about her movie role.

"I guess I shouldn't have gone to the strike," she admitted quietly.

"Says who?" Lily leaned closer and lowered her voice even more. "Listen, doll-baby, you made the world a little bit better by speaking out for what you believe in. Nobody can fault you for wanting to see more fairness in the world. Just remember that the best we can do in this life is follow our hearts."

Rebecca leaned gratefully into Lily's hug. *The best we can do in this life is follow our hearts.* Rebecca knew she had also followed her heart when she acted in the movie. She decided she wouldn't tell her family about that for a long, long time—if ever.

Aunt Fannie paced back and forth, holding a glass of tea absently. "If only Jacob and Josef are not hurt," she fretted.

"And if only Papa and Max have enough money to bail them out," said Rebecca's brother Victor. "If not, the court will sentence them to the workhouse."

"What about the goons—those men who hurt the strikers and hit me with a rock?" Rebecca asked. "Why aren't *they* in jail?"

"Because the city cares more about keeping the factories running than helping the workers," said

Michael with disgust. "The factory owners can get away with anything."

Sadie handed Rebecca a steaming glass. "Don't get excited," she said soothingly. "Drink some tea."

Sophie whispered, "I put in two lumps of sugar."

Footsteps sounded on the stairway, and everyone stared anxiously at the door. Max and Papa came in first, followed by Uncle Jacob and Josef. Aunt Fannie nearly spilled her tea as she ran to embrace her husband and son. They had dark circles under their eyes and angry purple bruises on their faces. Mama settled them comfortably in the parlor, while Aunt Fannie and Bubbie bustled about filling plates of food for them.

"How is the strike going?" asked Michael.

"There is one good result so far," Uncle Jacob answered. "The bosses are going to meet with the strike leaders. The owner of the coat factory has agreed to listen to their complaints and discuss solutions. The workers won't get everything they want, but some things should get better."

Rebecca's spirits lifted. The strike was working! Then she saw Uncle Jacob's shoulders slump. He buried his face in his hands. What was wrong? Even if the workers didn't get everything they wanted, wasn't it still a victory?

When Uncle Jacob looked up, his eyes were filled with despair. "There is one more thing. All the workers who were arrested have been fired. And they will make sure no other factory hires us either. We'll be labeled as troublemakers."

"Then what good did it do for us to strike?" Josef asked angrily. "It doesn't matter what improvements the bosses make—it won't help us!"

Rebecca saw Aunt Fannie's face cloud with disappointment, and tears trickled down Ana's cheeks. Uncle Jacob and Josef losing their jobs was exactly what they all had feared. Had they been wrong to support the strike?

"We had to try to make things better," Uncle Jacob said. "What else could we do?" He looked at Josef. "Remember, *tikkun olam*. Maybe the strike won't help you and me, but it will help all workers who come after us." Josef placed his hand on his father's shoulder, and Uncle Jacob pressed his own over it.

CHAPTER
FIVE
—

CHANGES IN THE AIR

Battery Park

"Hooray—today's the picnic at Battery Park!" Benny cried, clapping his hands together. Then he pouted. "But I won't get a haircut." He stamped his foot.

"Haircut?" Rebecca asked. "What makes you think you'd go to the park for a haircut?"

"Mama said there'll be a barbershop at the picnic," Benny answered. "But I don't want a haircut!"

Rebecca and her sisters giggled. "That's a barbershop *quartet*," Sophie explained patiently. "That means four men who sing songs in harmony. They aren't really barbers!" Benny looked puzzled.

"You'll hear them sing at the picnic," Mama said. "And don't worry, I definitely wouldn't let a singer cut your hair before your very first day of school." She smiled, but Rebecca thought Mama looked a bit wistful, almost as if she was sorry to see Benny start kindergarten.

"Labor Day always seems like the last day of summer to me," Sadie said. "Before you know it, school starts. No more lazy days!"

The weather had changed dramatically after the thunderstorm last week, and the air was refreshingly cool. Something else had changed, too—Uncle Jacob and Josef were out of work. Aunt Fannie talked about taking in a boarder to help pay the rent, but where would a boarder sleep in their cramped tenement?

At the entrance to Battery Park, Ana and her family joined Rebecca's family.

"How are you feeling?" Ana asked Rebecca. "Are you still dizzy?"

"Just a little. I won't be able to run in the three-legged race," Rebecca said. "But I'm lots better."

Ana breathed in deeply. "Don't you love the cool weather? I heard a peddler on Orchard Street

say the air is as crisp as a fresh apple." The girls
laughed.

The two families spread out
their blankets in a spot with a
good view of the bandstand.
The band members were
tuning their instruments, and
the many different notes added
to the festive commotion all around.

"Come on, Benny, let's go play catch," Victor
said, and Rebecca's brothers headed to an open
space on the grass.

Rebecca spotted Max and Lily arriving with a
group of people she recognized from the moving
picture studio. L.B. Diamond, the director who had
given her a part in his movie, looked dashing in a
sporty coat and high boots. And there was Roddy
Fitzgerald, the friendly studio carpenter who had let
her crank the phonograph at lunch that day. Rebecca
felt rather shy around the director, but she wanted
to say hello to Roddy.

The rest of her family was unpacking the picnic
lunch. "Mama, I see Max and Lily. I'll go get them,"
Rebecca said quickly. She got up and hurried toward

the group before Mama could tell her to sit still.

"How's the old bean?" Max asked, squinting at her forehead.

"Covered by the beanie," Rebecca quipped, pointing to her hat.

"Doll-baby, it's good to see you looking chipper again," said Lily. She turned to the director. "L.B., you remember my kid sister from *The Suitor*, don't you?"

"Ahh, the kidlet!" said L.B., shaking Rebecca's hand. "Who could forget those great big eyes?"

Rebecca felt herself blushing, pleased that he remembered her. "Hello, Mr. Diamond," she said politely. Then she turned to the carpenter. "Hi, Roddy." It was so good to see the whole crew again!

Roddy doffed his hat and gave a short bow. "Greetings, missy. I hear you had a bit of an adventure at the coat factory last week."

"Yes, I—I did," Rebecca stammered, taken by surprise.

"My wife's sister works at that self-same factory," Roddy went on. "She saw you start to give your speech. She says you're a mighty brave lass."

Rebecca's cheeks felt warm. She hadn't expected

anyone outside her family to know about the speech, but she was glad that Roddy approved.

Rebecca led Max and Lily to where the rest of the family had set out their blankets. Lily unpacked her basket and offered Max an array of tempting foods. Max beamed at Lily as each dish was laid out. Victor and Benny had returned and seemed to have worked up quite an appetite after their game. As everyone ate and chatted, the band played rousing patriotic songs that got the crowd clapping in rhythm. Then the musicians gave a drum roll as a stout man stepped to the front of the bandstand and held a megaphone to his mouth.

"That is Mr. Levy from the garment workers' union," Uncle Jacob told them. "He set up the meeting we went to."

"Labor Day became a national holiday twenty-one years ago," Mr. Levy began. His voice resonated across the park. "It was set aside as a day to honor all workers. Yet most factory workers will lose a full day's pay for taking today off for the holiday." The crowd booed.

The speaker lowered the megaphone and held up his hand to silence the audience. "But with every strike, some progress is made," he continued. "When workers and their families stand up for justice in spite of danger, people are forced to take notice. Just last week, a young lady stepped up to address the strikers at the Uptown Coat Company and was shamelessly attacked by thugs hired by the factory owners."

"Clara Adler," Rebecca whispered to Ana and Michael, and they nodded solemnly, remembering how the young speaker had been knocked from her soapbox and dragged away.

Mr. Levy kept talking. "I'm told that the brave little lady is here today, and we hope she will step forward and deliver the message that she was prevented from reading last week." The crowd clapped with enthusiasm. Rebecca looked around for Clara Adler, delighted that she would finally get to hear her speak. Mr. Levy's voice rang out again. "Will Rebecca Rubin please join me at the bandstand?"

Rebecca's family looked at her in astonishment, but nobody was more surprised than Rebecca. "What shall I do?" she mumbled.

"Your audience awaits you," Max said, helping Rebecca to her feet. "Get up there and wow 'em!"

Rebecca's head felt light, but it was from the surprise of the moment, not her injury. She picked her way through the crowd, and when she stepped onto the bandstand, Mr. Levy pumped her hand up and down and then motioned her to the front.

Rebecca had lost her letter in the melee at the strike, and she didn't know what to say. For a moment she simply stared at the expectant crowd. Gazing out at the upturned faces, Rebecca looked at her own family, gathered together on the grass. Her parents and grandparents, cousin Max, and Ana's family had all come to America for better lives. Now Uncle Jacob and cousin Josef had lost their jobs in the struggle for fair treatment. Rebecca realized she didn't need to read her letter. What she had to say was in her heart.

"When my uncle and cousin came to America," she began, "they got jobs in the coat factory and worked hard twelve hours a day. But the factory was a dark, dirty, dangerous place, and the bosses were very unfair to the workers. So my uncle and cousin joined the strike, hoping to make things better. They were fired from their jobs, but they didn't fail in their efforts. Finally, the bosses will make changes!"

People cheered. "Thanks to the strike, the factory will be a better place to work." Rebecca paused, remembering her uncle's words to Josef. "Maybe not for my uncle and cousin, but for all the workers who come after them." Applause erupted through the audience.

Rebecca felt as if another voice had come from her mouth. She hadn't known she could make a speech. Maybe that was part of being an actor. You could stand in front of an audience without being afraid, and give people something to think about, something to remember. Rebecca hoped she had done that today.

"Well, Rebecca," said Papa as she returned to the blanket, "you are a natural in front of a crowd. You're going to make a fine teacher someday." Mama nodded proudly.

"You're a girl with chutzpah," Grandpa exclaimed.

"I always said she was a born actress," Max commented.

Rebecca's head was spinning. If only she had the chutzpah to tell her parents that she wanted to be an actress—not a teacher.

Max cleared his throat. "I hate to move the spotlight, but I have some good news and some bad news to share." Everyone looked at him expectantly. "First the bad news—my movie studio, Banbury Cross, is moving to Hollywood, California."

"Oh, Max," Mama cried. "Have *you* lost your job, too?"

"Not at all," Max reassured her. "In fact, I'm going to be the studio's lead male actor—out in California."

"Is that good news," Mama sighed, "or bad news? I'm not sure which."

"What's so different?" Bubbie asked. "You move from one place to another, but always you come back."

"Not this time," Max said. "Hollywood's going to be my home. All the studios are moving out there. The weather is sunny and warm all year, perfect for shooting outdoors. California has every possible setting—mountains, deserts, forests, and ocean, as well as cities. Mark my words, this is just the beginning of something too big to even imagine. And I'm planning to be part of it."

Grandpa was shaking his head and smiling at

the same time. "What do you know? Whoever thought our Moyshe would amount to anything? But this Max——" He slapped Max on the shoulder. "Look at him, a real success. *Mazel tov!*"

Rebecca was stunned. Max was going to move across the whole country! She might never see him again—certainly not for a long time. Her voice quivered as she asked, "What about Lily?"

"That's the rest of the good news." Max smiled. "Lily's coming to California with me—or I'm going with her!" He took Lily's hand. "We're getting married first, and everyone is invited."

"A wedding!" Sadie and Sophie exclaimed.

"What wonderful news," Mama said. "Oh, Max, I'm so happy for you both."

Lily took a dainty diamond ring from her pocket and slipped it onto her finger. She held out her hand so everyone could admire the sparkling stone. "I hated to take it off, even for an hour," she said, "but I didn't want to spoil the surprise."

So that was the secret Lily had been saving for just the right moment. Rebecca realized she wasn't the only one who had been keeping a secret. But

"Are you moving to Hollywood, too?" Ana asked Roddy when the song ended.

Roddy shook his head. "It's supposed to be a regular paradise out there, but I won't be going."

"You'll be out of a job," Rebecca said. "What will you do?"

"I've always dreamed of having my own business," Roddy replied. "I want to build things that will last longer than a movie set. I'm starting my own construction company to build an apartment house in Brooklyn."

"Brooklyn!" Ana said. "Isn't that awfully far?"

"Not with the subway," Roddy answered. "People are moving out there as fast as housing can be built. It's a humdinger of an opportunity. My new building is going to have everything, including private bathrooms."

"Imagine having a real china bathtub inside your apartment!" Ana marveled.

"That's the idea." Roddy grinned. "I've got the land, and all I need to do is hire a good crew. I can't do everything myself, you know." He frowned. "I'm having a devil of a time finding a plumber, and good cabinetmakers are as scarce as leprechauns."

Rebecca's heart jumped. "I guess you need some-one who can make cupboards and shelving and—"

"—and carved mantelpieces," Ana added, catching Rebecca's eye.

"Indeed I do," Roddy said. "And where am I going to find such a man?"

"Ana and I know a fine cabinetmaker," Rebecca cried. "Come with us!" The girls each took one of Roddy's hands and led him to their family's blanket. "Roddy Fitzgerald, meet Jacob Rubin, your new cabinetmaker."

Uncle Jacob stood up to shake Roddy's hand, looking confused. "What is this all about?" he asked. The two men began to talk about carpentry, and in a few minutes, Roddy offered Uncle Jacob a job.

Uncle Jacob shook Roddy's hand warmly. "This is much more than I was making in coat factory," he said. "My son Josef, he could go to school." Then he hesitated. "This Brooklyn—it is far?"

"Well, it's a bit of a haul from here," Roddy admitted. "I plan to move out there. Maybe you'll want to settle there with your family so that you won't have to travel to get to work. The air is cleaner, and the rents are a good deal lower."

Once again, the family was full of smiles and congratulations as word of the new job spread. This time, Rebecca could share in the joy with everyone else.

The band began playing a lively folk tune, and people got up to dance. They formed a line that grew longer and longer as more people joined in. Soon the line began to snake around the park. Papa took Mama's hand and led her in, followed by Max and Lily and Uncle Jacob and Aunt Fannie. Rebecca's sisters and brothers and cousins linked hands and began to dance. Rebecca couldn't just sit and watch. She joined the line next to Ana and Michael and let the music move her feet.

When the dance ended, Max fell into step beside Rebecca as they walked back to the blanket. "I was awfully proud of you today," he said. "How did you like being on a stage again?"

Rebecca reflected for a moment. "Well, I'm glad I thought of something to say. But it wasn't as much fun as being in a movie."

"No, it's not the same at all," Max agreed. "There's a big difference between acting on a set and *taking* action. And you are certainly a lady of action!"

Rebecca joined the line next to Ana and Michael
and let the music move her feet.

Rebecca considered the difference. "You once said movies let people forget their troubles," she said at last. "But speeches can help people *solve* their troubles, can't they?"

Max nodded. "People like to get away from their worries for a while, and movies are wonderful for that. But there are times when we need to face problems head-on in order to fix them. That's what speeches can do."

When they reached the blanket again and Rebecca settled back down beside Papa, she knew there was one more speech she had to make. But she couldn't think of a way to start.

The band began playing a slow, lilting melody, and suddenly Rebecca thought of a way. "Papa, my teacher Miss Maloney once told us that America is a great melting pot," she began. "But I think America is more like a band. People play all different instruments, and together they make music." She looked around at her family. They were all listening. "Papa, your music is running the store and helping people who need shoes. Uncle Jacob's is building things out of wood. Bubbie's music is teaching us to cook and sew. As for me—my music is acting." She took a deep breath. "I don't want to be a teacher, Papa. That would be the wrong note for me." Now her words flowed faster. "When I visited Max's studio last spring, I got a part in the movie, and now I'm sure I want to be an actress."

Papa face darkened. "You acted in a moving picture—"

"—and you didn't tell *us?*" Sadie cut in.

"And you didn't invite us to *see* it?" Sophie added.

"You're in for it now," Victor said to Rebecca under his breath.

"Why, I—I—I declare!" Mama sputtered, fanning herself with her hand.

Bubbie shook her finger at Rebecca. "What were you thinking, not to tell your own family? What are we—nobodies?"

"This moving pitcher," Grandpa said sternly, "it's respectable?"

"Of course it is," Lily piped up. "*I'm* in it!"

"She's the star," Max said proudly. "In fact, we met on the set." He put his arm around Rebecca's shoulders. "The director is not easily impressed, but he thought our Rebecca was a natural talent."

Papa opened his mouth, and then clamped it shut without a word. Rebecca squirmed during the long silence until he finally spoke. "My Rebecca, acting in moving pictures? This I have to think about." Then Papa met Rebecca's eyes. "I guess it's true that we all play different instruments," he said slowly. "I have no doubt that whichever one you play, it's going to be heard by a lot of people. But as for this acting . . . well, I'll have to think about that."

Rebecca let out a long sigh. What a strange day it had been, with so many ups and downs. *Strange, but good*, she decided.

The bandleader made an announcement, and Ana jumped up. "It's time for the three-legged race!" She looked down at Rebecca. "How about if we just go watch?"

Rebecca shook her head. "I don't want to watch the race." Then she laughed and stood up, taking her cousin's hand. "I want to enter it!"

Mama lifted her eyebrows. "You've had a big day already, Rebecca. Are you sure you're up to it?"

Rebecca nodded. Suddenly, she felt she could do just about anything.

LOOKING BACK

CHANGES FOR AMERICA IN

A young stitcher and her boss in a clothing factory

When Rebecca was a girl, factory strikes were
common events. Of the millions of immigrants who
had recently come to America, a great many worked in
factories. At first, the immigrants were grateful to have
jobs, but soon they realized that the factory jobs were
trapping them in poverty. They worked long, hard hours
for little pay.

The Jewish religion teaches that all people are equal
and everyone deserves to be treated with dignity and
respect. But as Rebecca discovered, factory workers were
not treated like people—they were treated like machines
that could work twelve hours a day, six days a week.
They were treated as though their comfort, their health,
even their lives didn't matter.

Jewish immigrants, who had come to America
to escape *persecution*, or cruel treatment, found their

treatment in the clothing factories intolerable. Jews called America the *goldeneh medina*—the golden country— because they believed it was a land of freedom and opportunity. When they found something that didn't fit this ideal, they wanted to change it for the better.

Factory workers quickly learned that simply quitting a job did no good, because a job at another factory would be just as bad, and when one worker left, there were plenty more the factory could hire. But if *all* the workers in a factory walked out together, or went *on strike*, the owners might listen to the workers' demands. Striking, as Uncle Jacob and Josef did, was different from quitting, because the workers hoped to get their jobs back once the strike was over. Also, workers on strike didn't just go home. Instead, they stood outside the factory every day in a picket line, carrying signs that told the public why they were striking.

Sometimes picketers wore their signs!

Another way workers could get factory owners to listen to their demands was by joining a *union*, a type of workers' club whose leaders pressed the factory owners to improve conditions and wages. Factory owners didn't like unions, so workers often went on strike to be allowed to *unionize*, or join a union.

The workers who got the lowest pay and suffered the worst treatment in the clothing factories were teenage girls and young women, like the stitchers Rebecca saw. Their mistreatment drove some of them to become leaders in changing the factories.

Teenage girls in a Chicago factory

These girls and young women realized that although they were powerless alone, by working together they could bring about change. One young Jewish immigrant named Bessie Abramowitz led a walkout by 16 button sewers to protest their low wages at a Chicago factory. At first, nobody took the young women seriously—but within six weeks, most of the 8,000 workers at Bessie's factory had joined her, and soon other factories were shut down as their workers joined the strike.

To start a strike, leaders posted notices like this one in neighborhoods where the factory workers lived.

Gaining public support was an important part of a successful strike. Clara Lemlich, another young Jewish immigrant, led a strike of 20,000 girls and women that shut down many of New York's shirtwaist factories. For three months in the winter of 1909–1910, the young women stood shivering in the rain and snow. They were beaten by thugs and arrested by police, but still they stayed on the picket line. "There was never anything like it," said an observer. "An equal number of men would never hold together under what these girls are enduring." By the end, even wealthy women who didn't work for a living had joined the picket line to show their support. The strikers won shorter hours and higher wages, and they inspired other workers to fight for their rights.

Clara Lemlich

Some factories began to improve working conditions, but many did not. In 1911, a fire broke out

A newspaper story about the 1909 shirtwaist strike

Policemen arresting a woman striking at a Chicago clothing factory

in New York's Triangle shirtwaist factory. The owners had locked the exits to prevent the workers from stealing or leaving, and 146 workers died, trapped in the burning building.

After the Triangle fire, the public started demanding safety improvements, and New York state began passing laws to protect workers. Factory owners had to provide decent lighting, ventilation, bathrooms—and fire sprinklers. But it would take three more decades and many strikes by all kinds of workers—in coal mines, steel mills, shipyards, and factories—before Americans would have the labor standard we know today: a 40-hour work week and legal protection against unsafe conditions.

Young immigrants like Bessie Abramowitz and Clara Lemlich showed that one person's leadership and

Most of the Triangle factory workers were teenage girls and young women, nearly all of them Jewish and Italian immigrants.

determination can make a difference. When Rebecca saw the bad treatment of workers in the factory and on the picket line, she too was determined to speak out and try to change things for the better. After she grew up, Rebecca might have used her public-speaking skills to become a leader in the movement for workers' rights, as Clara Lemlich and Bessie Abramowitz did. If Rebecca became a movie actress, she would likely have joined the screen actors' union so that she would be paid fairly by the movie studios.

Jewish people have always deeply valued fairness, equality, and opportunity. In Rebecca's time, when millions of Jewish immigrants settled in America, they brought these values with them into the workplace and into American society. Like Rebecca, they were willing to stick up for the underdog and speak out for what's right. Many of their children and grandchildren went on to become leaders in the fight for people's rights.

Journalist Gloria Steinem (left),
Congresswoman Bella Abzug (center), and
Supreme Court Justice Ruth Bader Ginsburg (right)
have devoted their careers to women's rights.

ER America

GLOSSARY

chutzpah *(HOOTS-pah; first syllable rhymes with "foot")*—The Yiddish way of saying **boldness, nerve**

goldeneh medina *(GOL-den-eh meh-DEE-nah)*—In Yiddish, **golden country**—and this usually meant America!

mazel tov *(MAH-zl tof)*—Hebrew for **congratulations**

nu *(noo)*—a Yiddish expression with many meanings, often used like **"Well?"** or **"So tell me!"**

tikkun olam *(tee-KOON oh-LAHM)*—In Hebrew, **repair the world.** The Jewish belief that each person should do his or her part to make the world a better place